Georgia

"It is not so much for its beauty that the forest makes a claim upon men's hearts, as for that subtle something, that quality of air, that emanation from old trees, that so wonderfully changes and renews a weary spirit." ~Robert Louis Stevenson

Copyright ©2010 by Julia Heckathorn

Printed August 2011 in the United States of America

www.searchforthehiddenclover.com

Library of Congress Cataloging-in-Publication Data

Heckathorn, Julia
Search for the Hidden Clover: Redwood Forest / Julia Heckathorn
Summary: When two children and a kangaroo go searching for a four leaf clover in the Redwood Forest, they encounter fascinating animals and the tallest trees the world has ever known.

ISBN: 978-0-9837010-1-9

Library of Congress Control Number: 2011910493

This book is CPSIA compliant

Photo Credits: Pygmy Sloth photo- ©Bryson Voirin and Margaret D. Lowman, Ph.D. of the Tree Foundation, www.treefoundation.org
California Spotted Owl Photo- ©Sheila Whitmore from The Sierra Nevada Adaptive Management Project, http://snamp.cnr.berkeley.edu

Search for a clover, discover the world.

SEARCH FOR THE HIDDEN CLOVER

REDWOOD FOREST

WRITTEN AND ILLUSTRATED BY JULIA HECKATHORN

I went to a place
Where the **trees** were **so tall**,
They touched through the clouds,
And **made me feel small**.

As the Trees **grew in height**,
They **grew in width** too,
The biggest trees in the world,
I saw them, it's true!

And the **wildlife** there,
Was truly **unique**.
There were **Elk** in the **Meadows**,
Banana slugs by the creek!

A wonderful, **magical** place, **take a peek**!

Join us on an ADVENTURE into the REDWOOD FOREST in search of a 4-Leaf Clover!

CLOVERS aplenty
Of the GREEN clover kind
In a large clover patch
Is what we must FIND!

And in a large patch,
We **must** find a prize-
A clover with four leaves
With the **help** of keen eyes.

There's a
4-leaf
clover on this page!
Can you   find it?

③

BANANA SLUGS!

Top Tentacles- The large set on top senses light and movement. These tentacles act as the eyes.

Bottom Tentacles- The smaller set on the bottom is used for smell. These tentacles act as the nose.

IF A BANANA SLUG SENSES DANGER, HE PULLS HIS TENTACLES INTO HIS HEAD!

There are 5 Banana Slugs that sense danger! Can you find them?

"I'd be **happy** to **HELP**
For I know this place well.
I'm **Banana Slug Doug,**
And here's where I dwell."

"But it's **too muddy** and wet,
You won't find **clovers** here.
Let's go into the **forest**
And look for them there."

Boomeroo **hopped** in front
As we followed her lead.
But Jason **ran** off
With **WONDER** and speed.

Jason was **curious**,
Often looking for more
Than a **four-leaf** clover
On the forest floor.

7

So I
looked up
and saw
The most
magical tree!

Bigger than any tree
I'd imagined I'd **see**!

JULIA
SAYS
Coast Redwood trees can
grow to be 367 feet tall!
That's taller than the
Statue of Liberty!
And they can live to
be 2,000 years old!

9

And from there Jason **looked**
For the lowest tree limb,
To CLIMB up the tree
Like a big jungle gym.

He thought he could **see**
A clover from high,
But **he wished** he could get there
with **wings** that could fly.

Instead, with our help,
And **Boomeroo's jump,**

We tried so hard!...

It **couldn't** be reached,

And we fell with a **thump.**

Then a kind little **owl**
Flew down from up high,
Saying, "These trees grow higher
Than even **I** can **fly**!
They're the **TALLEST** of **trees**
The **world's** ever known,
So it's tricky to climb
A **Redwood** that's grown."

JULIA SAYS

The California Spotted Owl is endangered, and very hard to spot in the wild as they live in the deepest parts of the forest.

"And it's hard to see **CLOVERS**
From so very high,
But the **meadow**
Has a very big clover **supply!**"

⑬

There are 4 owls hiding in the forest!
Can you find them?

So out of the woods
To the **meadow** we walked,
Where we met a new **friend**,
A large **Elk** who talked.

(15)

A group of Elk is called a HERD!
In a HERD OF ELK, you may count up to 50 Elk!

There are 4 Elk that are facing the wrong way! Can you find them?

"Just HOP on my back, and in the meadow we'll see
If some clovers have four leaves,
                    or if they only have three."

18

We found lots of **clovers**
As we intently looked down,
And as we looked even **harder**,
A FOUR-LEAF CLOVER WAS FOUND!

Do you see the 4-leaf clover?

19

BUT WAIT! THERE'S MORE!

Have you ever seen a MARBLED MURRELET?
The Marbled Murrelet is a bird that lives high up in the trees of old growth forests!

There are 4 Marbled Murrelets in this book sitting on their nests high up in the Redwood trees.
Have you spotted them?
You may have to go back and look for them!

AND GET READY TO JOIN US
ON OUR NEXT ADVENTURE
WHEN WE TRAVEL TO A NEW PART OF THE WORLD
IN SEARCH OF ANOTHER 4-LEAF CLOVER!

Help Save the Pygmy Sloths!

There are estimated to be **only 300** Pygmy Three-Toed Sloths **left in the world.**
They are quickly disappearing.
The Hidden Clover team is working with the Tree Foundation to help save them.

Find out how you can help by going to
www.Searchforthehiddenclover.com/pygmysloths

A portion of the proceeds of this book go towards efforts to save the Pygmy Sloths.
To find out more about the Tree Foundation, go to www.TreeFoundation.org